I0830771

# Two Minutes of Heaven

# Two Minutes of Heaven

by Helen Hein

Illustrated by Linda Jacobus

y socialite mother and my new husband had a cool, aloof relationship, resembling disdain, until one special morning…

They didn't like each other very much. Not from the beginning, and not even after a few months. My mother, Jackie, and Scott, my husband of one year, had never exactly hit it off. You could probably even accurately describe their relationship as contentious.

My parents live in a nearby city, so while we see them fairly frequently, we aren't in each

others' pockets. Still, this in-law mutual friction between Mother and Scott only heightened when I announced my pregnancy. Scott, elated, couldn't wait for the sacred event, and Mother, at forty-nine, felt put out to the extreme to become a grandmother at such a young age. I'm twenty-three, and she thought I had oodles of time to start my family, and that I should have waited. Scott, at thirty-three, couldn't have disagreed with her more, and besides, as he noted, it was none of her business.

In my ninth month, my mother faced facts, and became accustomed to the idea of a baby in the family. Embracing layette shopping as a matter of familial duty, she in her usual manner of excess, went way overboard, supplying us with every useful and nonsense item ever produced for the younger set. Although I must admit, I especially loved the fabulous baby quilt she selected on one of her excursions.

"Doesn't she think I can support my own family?" Scott grumbled as he surveyed the latest loot in the nursery. By all accounts except Mother's,

Scott was a business success—albeit blue-collar— which was, sadly, the cause of her chagrin and discontent with her only child's spouse.

It's a bit easier to understand this prejudice when you're born with a silver spoon in your mouth as I was, but nevertheless, in my case the social status intolerance just didn't take. I love my carpenter. Wildly. There wasn't anybody on earth who could have kept us apart. Robert, my dad, loves him too, and that fact made the "bringing him home to meet the parents" step infinitely easier. It's also fortunate that my down-to-earth father

kept me from being too awfully spoiled rotten and biased. In fact, Dad was my hero, right up until I met Scott, and though my father didn't get dismissed in the love department, he did get usurped as hero.

Today I realized why it was such an easy, grace-ful transition of knight-in-shining-armor-hood from Dad to Scott. The two men are just plain alike. It frightened me, I admit, to also discover that in some ways, I take after my mother as well. In looks, this similarity is a blessed thing, because she's a beauty, and age has only increased

this marvel, but her somewhat stuffy personality and uptown attitudes are a tad bit scary for my decidedly laid-back country tastes. On occasion I have been known to interrupt myself with a mental swift kick when I catch a phrase of pomposity escaping my lips. What a puffball I used to be—and still am—now and then. Scott helps me with this. I sincerely hope I'm improving.

As they sometimes do, these things all came to my attention at once in a burst of awareness.

Shortly after the birth of my darling baby boy, on a crisp November evening, I had an open house at my fledgling, small town boutique to introduce an abundance of holiday selections. I feared that I had overspent my wad and overextended my energies, but once in a while, some unexpected happy thing takes place, as it did this night.

My open house turned out to be a full-blown social event, and Mother came to my rescue. With her interior design background, she was invaluable to me like never before. In short order, my little store looked sensational. Mother

transformed my rickety building, artfully covering the cracked wall with a golden Christmas tree brimming with elegant ornaments, and she disguised the worn carpeting with an elaborate layering of merchandise, giving the space such dimension and color that no one noticed where they stepped because the eye was drawn elsewhere to something beautiful.

As if this wasn't enough, her window displays beat all. Mother dressed a winter scene up in velvet and lace, in a manner befitting a grand old mansion, deserving of tender care and respect.

My mother and I wore long, luscious gowns for the occasion that were eye-popping for our casual, dressed-down husbands to view. Each and every woman who came to the store visibly relaxed as she walked in the door, greeted by us with a handshake or hug and a cup of hot apple cider. By eight, a regular party of women had gathered, sipping and chattering, enjoying the gentle music of the harpist we hired for the evening, the warm ambience of the many candles we had lit, and each other's company as they wandered through the store, touching and pointing at things.

I tired quickly, the unhappy result of getting up a time or two every night with my angel baby. Frankly, I was downright sleep-deprived and edgy. Rising to the occasion, however, Mother took over the bulk of my hostess duties with infinite finesse, and proceeded to sell a small fortune worth of merchandise. I was thrilled, as much as my irritable disposition would allow, and lavished profuse praise and my undying appreciation on her.

Did I mention that Mother brought a few of her wealthy friends from the city to indulge

their passion for shopping at my store that very evening?

It was truly a successful endeavor. My back room stock was depleted, and I was utterly exhausted by eleven when Mother mercifully walked the last, leisurely, night-owl customers to the door and flipped the sign to CLOSED, PLEASE COME AGAIN. I gained a new respect for Mom that evening, and fell asleep while extolling her exceptional virtues to my skeptical husband.

The next morning, however, blew my mind.

Babies are simply gorgeous little people, never accountable for waking up their mothers to nurse in the middle of the night or in the early hours of the morning. This morning was no different, only I was even more incoherent than usual because of my late and busy evening. Bobby, my beloved infant in fresh diapers, howled, as I, in my once-beautiful bathrobe, now showing signs of too many washings, carried him to the kitchen bar and slid gingerly into a chair to nurse yet again.

My precious husband ably built a fire, then loitered near the toaster, feebly attempting to help

my dad who had commandeered the kitchen to cook breakfast. Scott gratefully turned to observe his little family and smiled as he leaned down and slid his arms across the counter to us. "Lisa, honey, it should be a crime to look as good as you do in the morning without any sleep," he murmured in his low, deep voice filled with love.

Did I mention that my drop-dead handsome husband, who is virtually useless in the kitchen, is also exceedingly charming?

Suddenly, without any warning, it happened. Dad burst into song. Now, he has a nice voice, but not a great one. This day though, on a cold, rainy, early winter-like dawn, his singing sounded spectacular, and he chose of all things, a beach song! A surf's up type of number! I stole a glance at my mother across the room to gauge her reaction, and she looked nonchalant, busy working counting the proper number of place settings for our meal, while here was Dad, singing about the sun, the beach, and love at the top of his lungs. He sang and danced with total abandon, shimmying over to the breakfast

table with a plate of steaming bacon and sausage, where Mother didn't just set our plain Jane table, she prepared it as a thing of beauty, complete with exotic touches of branches and leaves she had collected earlier in the morning.

As Dad sidled up to her, singing and grinning about being on a blanket with his baby, he kissed the back of her neck. Mother, not terribly prone to overt displays of affection, smiled and kissed him back. Wonder of wonders! I think I even heard her giggle for a second or two. It was enough to melt an iceberg, and that wasn't all.

Duly inspired, my own husband, with an even more mediocre voice than Dad's, chimed in spontaneously to contribute harmony; his pathetic, off-key baritone offering the refrain. He is however, an incredible dancer, and this redeeming quality saved him from hilarity as he sensuously weaved his way around the breakfast bar to me and Bobby, gently cradling our baby's head as he moved, and stroking my cheek ever so tenderly. Bobby moved his head for a brief time to croon aloud too, and together my men made the most beautiful sounds that I've ever heard in the world.

It was two minutes of heaven, then it ended.

The song was over, the doorbell rang, and Mother's friends all piled into our smallish apartment for breakfast, while baby and I fled for the privacy of my bedroom to finish the feeding we started and to make ourselves presentable for company.

From that morning on, something perceptibly changed in the relationship between my mother and my husband. Perhaps they each gained a deeper appreciation for each other's finer qualities, or maybe Dad simply brought out the best in us

all by his great joy of life and complete lack of inhibition.

Whatever the case, I'll never forget those priceless moments, when three generations of a family melded into a seamless one—of love.

For additional titles by Helen Hein, please see
amazon.com/author/helenhein

Cover illustration for "Two Minutes of Heaven"
by Linda Jacobus, www.lindasart.com

**HELEN HEIN**, a Pacific Northwest author, poet, and artist, holds a Master of Arts Degree in Educational Psychology, and a Bachelor of Arts Degree in Communications. Helen worked several years as a mental health counselor, assisting families, teens, and children. Church work followed, as a pastoral staff minister for faith formation. Her first book, A COUNTRY PLACE, a contemporary love story and inspirational novel, is available in both traditional and e-book formats.

Currently, she writes on ideas, creativity, life planning, and transforming lives in a fast-moving

world, with IDEAS FOR WOMEN ONLY, The Art of a Personal Portfolio. Her uplifting short stories, like TWO MINUTES OF HEAVEN, offer hope for hectic lives. The success of starting a church quilt club from scratch inspired her to share how to do it. You can too, with her short e-book, SECRETS OF A SUCCESSFUL QUILT CLUB, A Ministry Model.

Married since 1980, with a grown son and daughter, she grew up on a large beef ranch with eight brothers and two sisters, the ninth of eleven children.

**LINDA JACOBUS** is owner of Linda's Witness in Art, Classical Realism Oil Paintings by Linda Jacobus. Linda was born in Palo Alto, California, and was raised in Saratoga until the age of eleven, eventually  moving to Martinez, California with her family of six sisters and one brother. Linda married and has four precious sons. In 2003, she and her husband moved to the beautiful Northwest, where she still resides.

Throughout her life, Linda had been searching to fill an unknown void. In 1992, she picked up a

brush and stroked the canvas, knowing then that the void had been filled. She is a self-taught artist and loves to study as much as she loves to paint. Being self-taught has enabled her to accomplish techniques in which she can freely express herself. She considers herself a tonalist, and enjoys depicting the unique degrees of value. Most of all, she loves to capture the light that shines upon the subject and the shadows that bring forth the light.

Linda has won awards, and has paintings throughout the country and abroad. In Linda's words, "I have come to the conclusion that what I paint God has created, I just copy His works. He is my teacher."